Meg and Jack's New Friends

Paul Dowling

Houghton Mifflin Company
Boston 1990

For Alick

Rosie

and

Guy

Copyright © 1989 by Paul Dowling
First American edition 1990
Originally published in Great Britain in 1989 by William Collins Sons & Co. Ltd.

Library of Congress Cataloging-in-Publication Data

Dowling, Paul, 1953-
  Meg and Jack's new friends / Paul Dowling.
      p.   cm.
  Summary:Having just moved into a new house, Meg and Jack first
shyly, then happily, get to know the children next door.
  ISBN 0-395-53513-1 (U.S.)
  [1. Moving, Household – Fiction.   2. Friendship – Fiction.]
  I. Title.
PZ7.D755Me   1990
[E]-dc20
                                                                          89-24450
                                                                             CIP
                                                                             AC

Printed in Belgium by Proost International Book Production

10 9 8 7 6 5 4 3 2 1

Chapter 1
WAITING

Meg and Jack have moved into a new house.
They are waiting for the children next door.

"When will they be here?"
asked Jack.

"In a minute," said Mom.

"I'd better get my bike out,"
said Jack, "and my ball,
and my new computer game.
I expect they'll want to play
with everything."

Jack lined up his things.

Meg ran into her bedroom.
She got her fire engine, her ball,
her new hat and all her best things.

She quickly hid
everything behind
the big armchair.

"I don't want them
to play with my
things," she said.

"They're here!
They're here!"
shouted Jack.

Coming up the path were Mrs. Diamond
and her two children, Rosie and Guy.

"Up, Mommy, up!" said Meg.

Mom took Meg's hand.
"Come on," she said. "Let's go and
open the door."

Chapter 2
PEEPING

"Hello," said Mom.
"Hello," said Mrs. Diamond.
"Hello," said Jack and Rosie.

"I've got a new ball," said Guy.
"What a lovely big red ball,"
said Mom.

Meg peeped under Mom's arm.

Rosie was a bit shy.

"Do you want to try my new
computer game?" asked Jack.

Rosie had never played on a
computer before.
"I'll show you how to do it," said Jack.

"Bleep! Bleep!" said the computer.

Mom and Mrs. Diamond had a cup
of coffee.
"Are you going to play with Guy, Meg?"
asked Mom.

Meg hid behind the chair.

"Guy wants to play ball," said Mom.

Meg disappeared under the table.

Guy found some of Meg's toys.
He telephoned the fire brigade,

squashed a space monster

and marched to London, blowing a trumpet.

Meg just peeped.

Chapter 3
WATCHING

Woooooooooosh
Jack and Rosie flew past.
"We're going on the bikes!"
they shouted.

Up and down.
Round and round.
In and out.

Jack and Rosie whizzed round the garden.

Guy wanted to ride.

"Where's your fire engine, Meg?"
asked Mom.
Meg quickly ran to the big armchair.

"I don't want Guy to have my fire engine," she said.

"Guy doesn't want to keep your fire
engine," said Mom.
"He just wants a ride on it."

Meg and Guy and Mom
took the fire engine
outside. Guy put his big
red ball in the back.
"Nee naw, nee naw," said Guy.

"Get your scooter, Meg," said Mom.

"Wait for me!" shouted Guy.

Rosie and Guy followed Jack all around the garden.

Meg just watched.

Chapter 4
FRIENDS

Crash!
Guy bashed into the wall.
"Wam, bang, bong!" shouted Guy.

He started laughing.

Rosie and Jack laughed.
Mom and Mrs. Diamond laughed

and Meg began to giggle.
She giggled and giggled.

Guy's big red ball had bounced out of
the fire engine.
Meg picked it up and gave it back to him.

She looked at Guy and giggled.
"Your hat's on the wrong way."

"Piddly pong," said Guy.

And they ran off together, laughing.

Meg and Guy telephoned the fire brigade,

squashed a space monster

and marched to London, blowing trumpets.

Root-de-toot.

"We have to march home now,"
said Mrs. Diamond.
"Can we play tomorrow?" asked Meg.
"You can come to our house,"
said Guy and Rosie.

"Great," said Jack.
"Wam, bang, bong!" said Meg.

F
DOW

Dowling, Paul.

Meg and Jack's new friends.

$10.70

DATE			